Medical Adventures with Dr. Andre...

A Violi... the Shed

Alisa,
I hope you enjoy my b
Never stop reading!
♡ Dr. Ham

by Dr. Kendra K. Ham

Illustrations by Mike Motz

Medical Adventures with Dr. Andrea

A Violin in the Shed

To my besties, Aundrea and Michelle,
who were both an inspiration for this book and series.

For all children and their parents
who want to learn more about the world of medicine.

The information in this book should not replace
seeking attention from a medical provider.

One hot summer day, Michelle decided to embark on an adventure. She was really bored. She had read books, ridden her bicycle, and watched TV, because none of her friends were able to come over to play. She even took a little ***siesta*** after lunch and the day still dragged on.

Siesta means **nap** in Spanish.

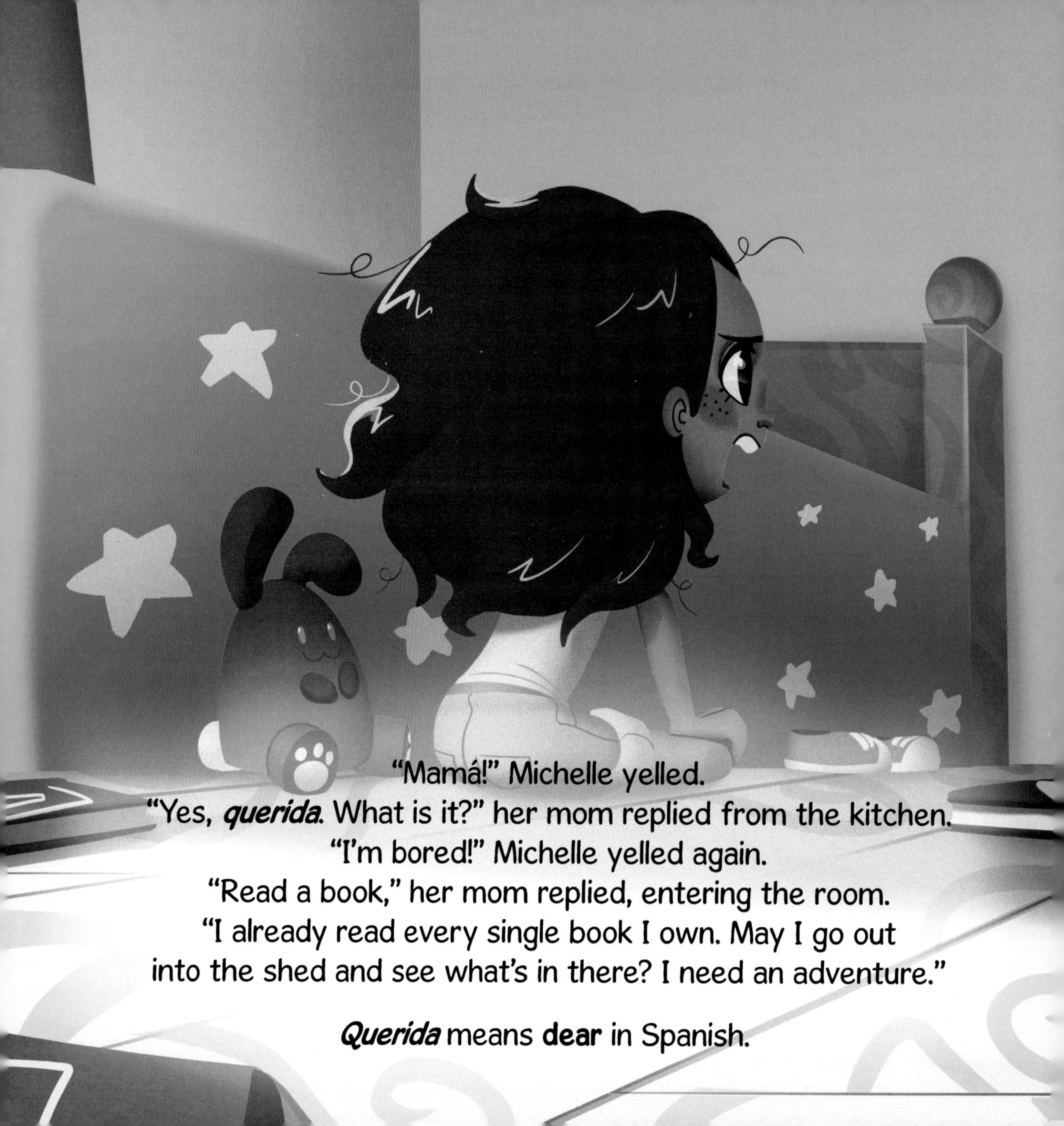

"Mamá!" Michelle yelled.
"Yes, ***querida***. What is it?" her mom replied from the kitchen.
"I'm bored!" Michelle yelled again.
"Read a book," her mom replied, entering the room.
"I already read every single book I own. May I go out into the shed and see what's in there? I need an adventure."

Querida means **dear** in Spanish.

“Absolutely not. I’m incredibly busy right now, and you are not allowed to go in the shed alone. You will have to wait until your father comes home from his work trip this weekend. There are probably spiders in that shed, and it will be dark soon,” her mom replied, walking back to the kitchen.

"Aw man," Michelle complained.

"Woof!" Michelle's dog, ***Amigo,*** looked up at Michelle as though complaining of boredom as well.

Michelle looked down at Amigo and said, "Let's sneak in there together. I don't want to wait until this weekend to have fun."

Amigo means **friend** in Spanish.

Michelle told her mom she was going to play in the backyard with Amigo. Her mom had no idea Michelle had other plans in mind. Michelle crept up to the storage shed as if she were on a secret mission for the FBI. It was definitely a secret, because if her mom found out, Michelle would be in big trouble. She put her finger to her lips and said, "Shhh," to Amigo so he wouldn't bark and blow their cover.

The shed was filled with old boxes and lawn equipment. There were spider webs everywhere. Behind one of the boxes, Michelle found a funny shaped case. She opened the case, and inside was her grandfather's old violin! Excited about her new discovery, she ran back into the house, not realizing she had company on the violin case. She started to feel a little itchy on her arms and legs, but this didn't stop her.

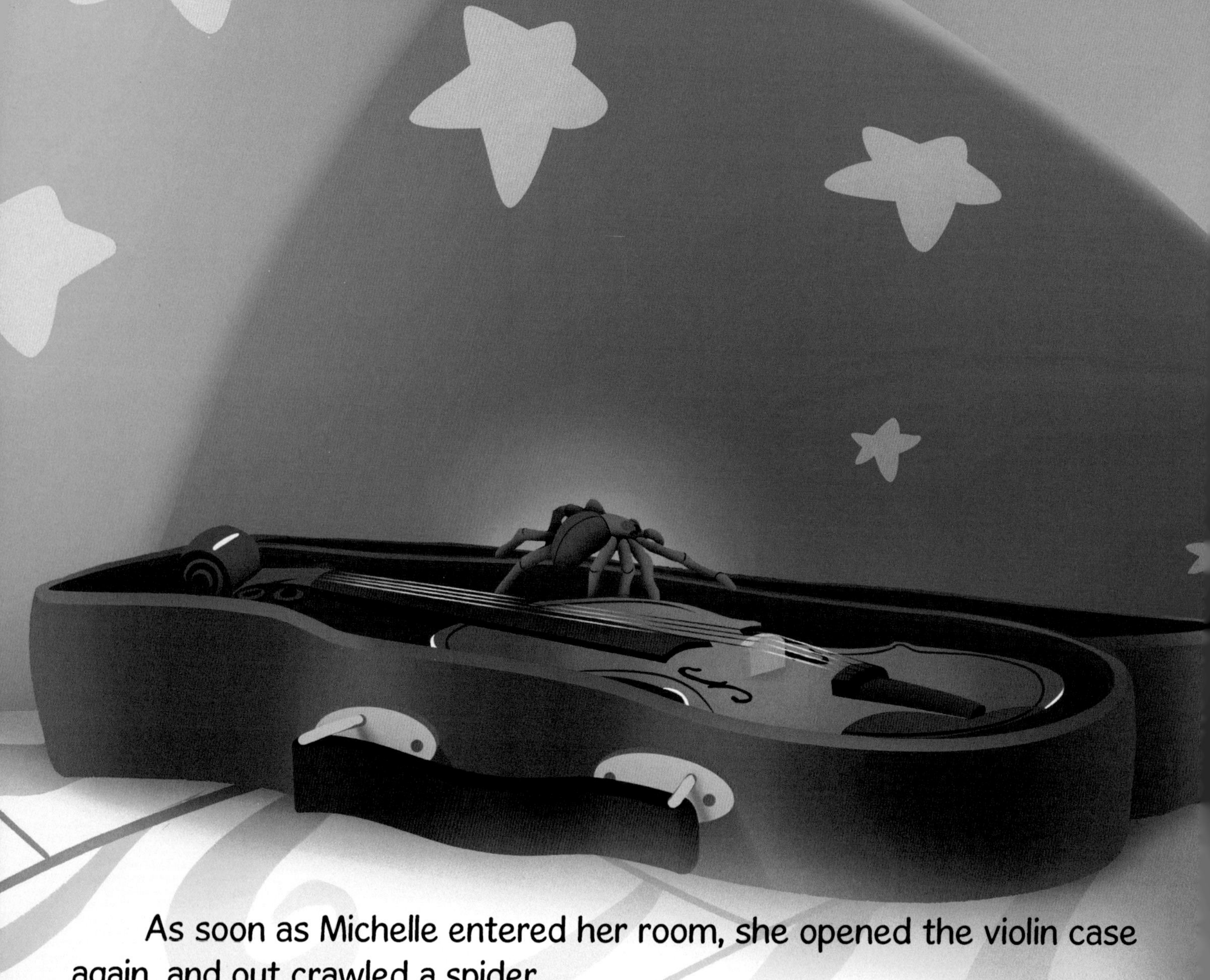

As soon as Michelle entered her room, she opened the violin case again, and out crawled a spider.

"Eek!" she shrieked, surprised by the spider.

Amigo started barking and ran after the spider. Michelle ran around her room, found an empty Play-Doh container, and caught the spider, using the lid to scoop him up.

She closed the lid on the container tightly and left it on the dresser so that she could go and eat dinner with her mom. After dinner, she checked on her spider again. She poked holes in the lid to make sure he could breathe. In the morning, she would do some research to learn more about her spider. She had no idea what he would want to eat for breakfast.

The next morning, scratching her arms the whole way, she ran into the kitchen to ask her mom what kind of spider she had caught.

"Aaahhh!!!" her mom screamed, dropping a dish to the floor, which shattered into several pieces. "What are you doing with that? Wait, that looks like..., Oh my goodness. That is a brown recluse spider!"

"A brown excuse spider?" Michelle asked.

"A brown recluse spider. They bite. What are those spots on your arms?" Michelle's mom asked.

"I think something bit me. My arms and legs are really itchy," Michelle replied.

"Did that spider bite you? Oh, no. We have to go to the doctor right away," her mom exclaimed.

Michelle's mom grabbed her and the Play-Doh container and got into the car. They headed to Dr. Andrea's office with the spider along for the ride, leaving poor Amigo out of the rest of the adventure.

There was a long wait at the doctor's office. Michelle's mom was quite worried that her daughter would need immediate attention. "My daughter was bitten multiple times by a brown recluse spider. Somebody do something, please!"

"We will take her back as soon as we can," the ***triage nurse*** replied.

A triage nurse is a nurse who is responsible for assessing the patient first and determining the need for immediate medical attention.

Once they were in the exam room, Michelle opened the lid of the Play-Doh container to examine the spider.

"Michelle, please put that thing away until the doctor comes in," her mom pled.

"Hey, everyone," Dr. Andrea greeted Michelle and her mom. "Michelle, I heard you might have been bitten by a spider?"

"I never saw the spider on me. He was just crawling around on my grandfather's violin case yesterday," Michelle replied.

"Dr. Andrea, she got several bites on her arms after being out in that shed yesterday, after I told her not to go out there," Michelle's mom complained.

"Oh, I see. You were on a little adventure?" Dr. Andrea smiled. Dr. Andrea looked at Michelle's arms and saw several raised pink bumps on her arms and legs. It looked like she had been scratching. Dr. Andrea didn't seem to be worried. Michelle's mom didn't understand why she was the only one concerned.

“Wanna see the spider, Dr. Andrea?” Michelle asked.

“Of course,” Dr. Andrea replied. She looked in the container and examined the spider with a magnifying glass. “Well, that is definitely a brown recluse spider. Do you know how you can tell? Brown recluse spiders have a mark shaped like a violin on their bodies, and they have six eyes.”

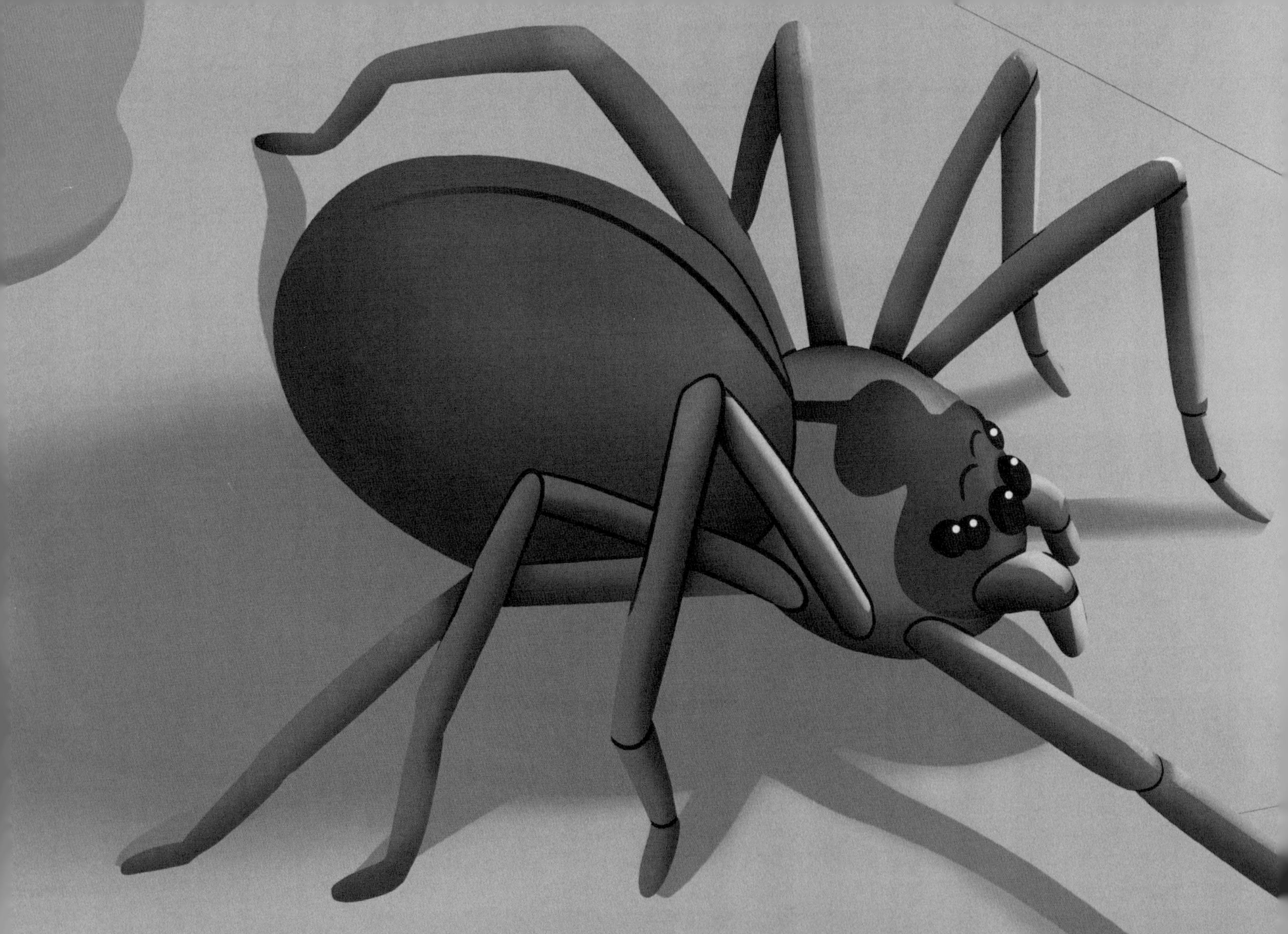

Dr. Andrea showed Michelle the features with the magnifying glass since the eyes were so small. "And yes, they can bite. Brown recluse bites usually start out a little red with two little marks in the center. Sometimes, over a few days, the bite can become darker and even turn blue if it gets worse."

Michelle and her mom listened closely. Michelle was really enjoying learning about her new friend.

Dr. Andrea continued, “And they like to hide in dark places, like that shed. They usually don’t bite unless they are scared you are about to hurt them. The bite doesn’t usually hurt either. A few hours after the spider bites, you may start to feel sick, throw up, have pain, and fever, or even muscle aches. But it looks like you just have mosquito bites. I don’t see any brown recluse spider bites.”

"Wow, what a relief." Michelle's mom sighed, sinking down in her chair with her hand over her forehead.

"I think it's cool. That's why he was on the violin case! He likes violins because he has one on his body!" Michelle exclaimed. Dr. Andrea chuckled.

"I'm glad you find all of this so amusing. I still don't want that spider anywhere near me," Michelle's mom said, with some concern in her voice.

"Just be careful out in that shed, Michelle. It is best if you don't go out there alone. Use some anti-itch cream as needed to help with the itching, and come back if you have any of the problems that we discussed," Dr. Andrea advised.

As they left, Michelle let the spider go into the bushes. Her mom shivered, glad she wouldn't see it again.

On the way home, Michelle wondered if the spider would find another violin case to call home.

Meet Dr. Kendra K. Ham

Kendra K. Ham, MD is a double board certified pediatrician and the medical director of two Children's Advocacy Centers in North Carolina. She enjoys working with children and parents to further their understanding of pediatric illnesses. Her hobbies include playing the piano, collecting earrings, traveling, and reading.

Made in the USA
Columbia, SC
31 July 2019